KEEP OUT

BEAST FEAST

BY EMMA YARLETT

One very HUNGRY day,
BEAST caught DINNER.
Beast was ever so pleased.
Dinner looked VERY TASTY.

"YOU are DINNER," said BEAST.

"No I'm not," said Dinner.

Beast didn't think he should keep such a TASTY DINNER all to himself. So he invited all of his BEASTLY FRIENDS to a BEAST FEAST.

Dinner looked worried.

Soon, Beast had his first reply.

Beast was very pleased that Sir Gutguzzler
could make it. He had a GREAT PLAN to
fatten up Dinner when...

Dinner had an IDEA! "Mr BEAST!" said Dinner. "This swill looks ... LOVELY. But how about some DELICIOUS CHOCOLATE CAKE? It would make me FAR plumper!"

PUTRID SWILL

Beast wasn't sure.

He'd never tried
CHocolate Cake before.

But it turned
out to be...

VERY TASTY indeed!
They stayed up all night
eating and snacking. Beast hoped Dinner
would be PLUMP enough for Sir Gutguzzler.

In the morning another BEAST replied.

Sealed with a

Beast couldn't WAIT to see madame GARgoyle.
He hadn't seen her since the MIDDLE AGES!
He had just found the salt grinder when ...

Beast had NEVER been
swimming in the SEA before.
The water was cold but ...

he had a WONDERful DAY!

He hoped Dinner
would be SALTY
enough for darling
Madame Gargoyle.

Soon there was MORE post.

MISTER
BEASTIE

Beast almost wished he hadn't invited
GIANT GRUMBO, but he went and
switched on the SLIME anyway.
Luckily Dinner had another IDEA!

"OH NO BEAST!" said Dinner. "That's nowhere near SLIMY enough. For extra slime and MUD there's only one place to go: the SWAMP!"

BEAST did love the swamp.
And Dinner's ideas had been VERY GOOD so far, so ...

OFF THEY WENT to the SWAMP.

The SLIMY slide was EXTRA fun!

Although Beast thought Dinner
PROBABly was muddy and
slimy enough for
the GIANTS...

he was beginning to wish he
didn't have to EAT Dinner.

Another day brought another BEASTly reply.

BEAST scratched his nose. His guests
were making such difficult demands.
What could he do to CHILL Dinner?
Then Dinner had an IDEA!

"LOOK outside my BEASTly FRIEND! Let's chill ourselves in the SNOW and build SNOW MONSTERS!"

Beast thought that sounded PERFECT.

It was the
BEST DAY.

At last it was the evening before the BEAST FEAST. Dinner had been PLUMPED and SALTED and MUDDIED and CHILLED. But Beast REALLY didn't want to eat Dinner tomorrow.

"You don't LOOK like Dinner any more."

"You don't look like such a BEAST any more..."

What could
they do?
Beast thought
and _thought_.
Could Dinner RUN?
Could Dinner HIDE?
But then all the BEASTS
would be ANGRY.
There was nothing for it.
"I'll just have to
SERVE DINNER,"
thought Beast.

The following day the BEASTS arrived one by one. They were VERY HUNGRY indeed and were looking forward to eating Dinner. Beast greeted them all warmly.

"Come inside!" said BEAST.
"I've been cooking for HOURS. DINNER IS SERVED!"

And DINNER had a rather good time too.